W9-BMZ-781

Dear Parents:

Congratulations! Your child is taking the first steps on an exciting journey. The destination? Independent reading!

STEP INTO READING® will help your child get there. The program offers five steps to reading success. Each step includes fun stories and colorful art or photographs. In addition to original fiction and books with favorite characters, there are Step into Reading Non-Fiction Readers, Phonics Readers and Boxed Sets, Sticker Readers, and Comic Readers—a complete literacy program with something to interest every child.

Learning to Read, Step by Step!

Ready to Read   Preschool–Kindergarten
• big type and easy words • rhyme and rhythm • picture clues
For children who know the alphabet and are eager to begin reading.

Reading with Help   Preschool–Grade 1
• basic vocabulary • short sentences • simple stories
For children who recognize familiar words and sound out new words with help.

Reading on Your Own   Grades 1–3
• engaging characters • easy-to-follow plots • popular topics
For children who are ready to read on their own.

Reading Paragraphs   Grades 2–3
• challenging vocabulary • short paragraphs • exciting stories
For newly independent readers who read simple sentences with confidence.

Ready for Chapters   Grades 2–4
• chapters • longer paragraphs • full-color art
For children who want to take the plunge into chapter books but still like colorful pictures.

STEP INTO READING® is designed to give every child a successful reading experience. The grade levels are only guides; children will progress through the steps at their own speed, developing confidence in their reading. The F&P Text Level on the back cover serves as another tool to help you choose the right book for your child.

Remember, a lifetime love of reading starts with a single step!

To Genevieve

These Are My Pets book, characters, text, and images © 1988, 2019 Mercer Mayer

Little Critter, Mercer Mayer's Little Critter, and Mercer Mayer's Little Critter and Logo are registered trademarks of Orchard House Licensing Company.

All rights reserved. Published in the United States by Random House Children's Books, a division of Penguin Random House LLC, 1745 Broadway, New York, NY 10019, and in Canada by Penguin Random House Canada Limited, Toronto. Originally published in different form as *Little Critter's These Are My Pets* by Golden Books, New York, in 1988.

Step into Reading, Random House, and the Random House colophon are registered trademarks of Penguin Random House LLC.

Visit us on the Web!
StepIntoReading.com
rhcbooks.com
littlecritter.com

Educators and librarians, for a variety of teaching tools, visit us at RHTeachersLibrarians.com

ISBN 978-1-9848-3099-9 (trade) — ISBN 978-1-9848-9495-3 (lib. bdg.) —
ISBN 978-1-9848-3100-2 (ebook)

Printed in the United States of America
10 9 8 7 6 5 4 3 2 1

This book has been officially leveled by using the F&P Text Level Gradient™
Leveling System.

Random House Children's Books supports the First Amendment and celebrates the right to read.

THESE ARE MY PETS

BY MERCER MAYER

Random House New York

This is my frog.

He is green.

He likes to sit in water.

I like to sit in water.

My frog is my friend.

This is my turtle.

He is green, too.

He likes to hide
in the grass.
I like to hide
in the grass.
My turtle is my friend.

This is my fish.

My fish is yellow.

She likes to swim.

I like to swim.

I like to look
at my fish.
My fish likes
to look at me.

My fish is my friend.

This is my dog.

My dog is brown

and white.

My dog likes to run.

I like to run.

My dog likes to dig.

I like to dig.

My dog is my friend.

This is my kitten.

She is black and white.

She likes my dog.
She likes his tail
best of all.

My kitten likes

my frog, too.

My kitten likes
to sit in the sun.
I like to sit
in the sun.
My kitten is my friend.

This is my bug.

My bug is black.

My bug likes to fly.

I like to see

my bug fly.

My bug likes

to sit on my hand.

I keep my bug in a jar.

I like my bug.

My bug is my friend.

This is my snake.

My snake is green

and yellow.

I keep my snake
in a cage.

My snake can move fast.

I can move fast.

My snake is my friend.

When I take a bath,
my friends want
to take a bath, too.
But Mom says, "No."

When I get in bed,
my friends get in bed, too.
But Mom says,

"No. No pets in bed.
Just say good night
and go to sleep."

So my frog says good night.

My dog says good night.

My kitten says good night.

My other friends do not

say a thing.

I say good night
to my friends.
And we all go to sleep.